Everybody Loves
To
Read to Me

This book is dedicated to all children.

Everybody Loves
to
Read to Me

Written by Ruby V. Shaffer

Illustrated by Jasmine Mills

Printed in the United States of America
Library of Congress Catalog Number: 2019939652
ISBN: 978-0-578-49613-9

My Mom read to me while I was in her womb.
The doctor told her that research says,
It's never too soon.

I bet I said,
"Yes, yes, yes, yes, what will it be?
My dear Mommy is reading to me!"

She said whatever she was reading,
She would read out loud.
Giving me a head start made
Mommy very proud.

It really made a difference,
Because I'm smart for my age.
I can even read...an entire page!

Dad read to me the other day.
I had more fun than when I play.

Dad changed his voice and made roaring sounds.
My little brother started spinning round and round.
When Dad was finished I wanted more.
The book he read was about giant dinosaurs.

Then I said,
"Yes, yes, yes, yes, what will it be?
Please Daddy read more to me."

Dad read to me one more time.
The book was almost like this one,
Full of rhythm and rhymes.

Grandma called me the other day.
She said she just wanted to say hey.

Then I said,
"Yes, yes, yes, yes, what will it be?
Please Grandma won't you read to me?"

So my Grandma read me a story,
Over the telephone.
Her stories are not short, they are very long.

I could hear the love in her voice...so soft and sweet.
As I sat quietly listening, in my seat.

My Papa stopped by to see my new pup.
I ran to his arms and he picked me up.
He gave me a hug
With a huge smile on his face.
Then he said, "Ready set go,"
And we began to race.

I ran to my room and got him a book.
He gave me a smile...I just love that look.

Then I said,
"Yes, yes, yes, yes, what will it be?
Papa, Papa please read to me."

Papa read to me...my favorite fairy tale.
I love his different impressions,
He does them so very well.

He made a sound just like a horse.
He's my favorite Grandpa,
But you know that of course.

I asked my big brother to read me a story.
He's really a neat brother, his name is Corey.
He said he was busy and didn't have the time.
I said, "Please big Brother, just one line."

Then I said,
"Yes, yes, yes, yes, what will it be?
Big Brother will you read to me?"

So he stopped what he was doing and opened the book.
I think he really liked it, he was really hooked.

The book told a story about the development of pearls.
How they are formed...is out of this world!

My favorite Auntie is really the best.

She always has a surprise for me, but makes me guess.

She loves reading to me, so I know it's a book.

She even bought me one to help me learn how to cook.

Her passion to get children reading is truly a gift.

It's really inspiring and she loves to uplift.

She's always ready, with books in her hands.
And yes, yes, yes, yes, I'm her biggest fan.

Then I said,
"Yes, yes, yes, yes, what will it be?
My favorite Auntie loves to read to me!"

My amazing Uncle reads to me.
But he only does so, when his schedule is free.

He always makes me laugh...when he reads.
And he constantly tells me...I will succeed.

Then I said,
"Yes, yes, yes, yes, what will it be?
My Uncle loves to read to me!."

My elderly neighbor lives next door.
She always give me cookies...sometimes four.

When her children were young she read every night.
Just before she turned off the lights.
Now that they are grown and on their own.
She says sometimes she feels all alone.

So she loves when I come out to play.
She knows exactly what I'm going to say.

Then I say,
"Yes, yes, yes, yes, what will it be?
My dear neighbor won't you read to me?

She reads the same story every time.
I know it by memory and really don't mind.

My best friend and I love to play.
We're outside together almost everyday.

We built a tent in the backyard.
My new puppy is the tent's special guard.

We love to jump, shout, and play.
We also make things out of dirt and clay.

The tent is full of books and lots of toys.
But when we read it's quiet...no noise.

So when we get tired we pull out some books.
Reading is just so much fun,
We're both very hooked.

Then I said,
"Yes, yes, yes, yes, what will it be?
Even my best friend loves to read to me!"

My teacher reads stories to the class everyday.
She reads to us right after we play.
I've learned so much from listening as she reads.
She said reading to children is like
Planting knowledge seeds.

Then I said,
"Yes, yes, yes, yes, what will it be?
It's very important to read to me!"

She said reading is more than words on a page.
It's a comprehension skill that develops with age.

Understanding what you read is really the key.
So please pick up a book everybody
And start reading to me!

My Sister read to me at a quarter to eight.
Mom said, "It's time to go to bed, it's getting late."
Sister said, "Five more minutes the book is great."
Mom said, "Okay Sister, but not too late."

Then I said,
"Yes, yes, yes, yes, what will it be?
My big Sister is reading to me!"

The books she reads to me are always funny.
I really enjoyed the one about the bunny.

The bunny thought he was a black and white cat.
Can you actually believe that?

Mom and Dad read to me just last night.
Then they gave me a hug and held me tight.
After they finished they tucked me in bed.
And you know exactly what I said.

"Yes, yes, yes, yes, what will it be?"

Mom said, "A purple bumble bee?

Dad said, "A talking oak tree?"

Then I said,
"Yes, yes, yes, yes, what will it be?
Everybody loves to read to me!"

The End...

No...

A New Beginning